For: Maisey

Rockpool Children's Books
15 North Street
Marton
Warwickshire
CV23 9RJ

First published in Great Britain by Rockpool Children's Books Ltd. 2012
Text and Illustrations copyright © Sam Walshaw 2011
Sam Walshaw has asserted the moral rights
to be identified as the author and illustrator of this book.

Printed in China

Sam Walshaw

Maisey and the Pirates
The
Ghost Ship

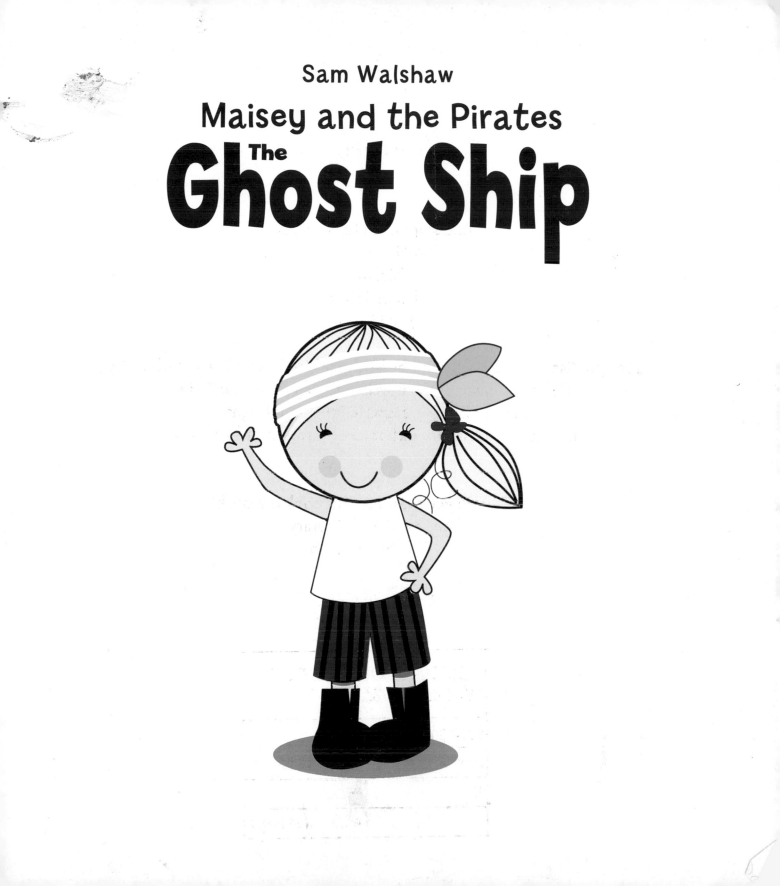

As usual, Captain Codeye and his pirates
were on the lookout
for some real pirate treasure.

"Arrr," said Captain Codeye,
thumbing through his pirate book.
"Let's look for the treasure of Captain Pinkbeard,
the most fearsome girl pirate
ever to have sailed the seven seas."

The pirates listened as Captain Codeye
told them Pinkbeard's story.
"She still roams the seven seas
in her ghost ship, haunting
any pirate who would try to steal her treasure."

The pirates didn't believe in ghosts,
but they did believe in treasure.

"Arrr,"
they yelled.
"What are we waiting for? Let's go!"

Maisey's little sister Milly wanted to join in the adventure. "Can I come too?" she begged. **"Pleeease!"**

"No, you can't, Milly," said Maisey, firmly.

"A trip like this is only
for **BIG** pirates, and you are
just a very **small** pirate."

"Ohhh," said Milly.
But she wasn't going to take no
for an answer. "I'll show them," she thought.

As the pirates sailed away, they tried
to imagine Pinkbeard's treasure.

"I wonder what the treasure will be?" said Daisy.
"I bet it's diamonds," said Maisey.
"I think it's gold," said Kearan.

While the pirates worked hard
on deck, Daisy went to
make a midnight snack,
to keep them going until morning.

All alone in the galley,
Daisy made jam sandwiches
and poured milk for all the pirates.
"This is their favourite midnight snack,"
she thought.

But as Daisy turned to go up on deck,
a ghostly figure floated by the door.

"Ahhh!" she screamed,
dropping jam sandwiches and milk everywhere.
She ran as fast as she could
back to the other pirates.

"Whatever's wrong, Daisy?" asked Kearan.
"I s-s-saw the ghost of Pinkbeard," gasped Daisy,
"Sh-sh-she was in the galley!"

"Don't be silly Daisy, there are
no such things as ghosts!" laughed Kearan.

"But I **DID** see her!" shouted Daisy.
"She was there!"

"Hmmm...
better just check,"
thought Kearan.

He climbed up to the
crow's-nest and peered through
his telescope for any sign of
Pinkbeard
and her ghost ship.

Suddenly, he heard a strange noise.

"Whooo...ooo..."

Then he felt an icy hand
touch the back of his neck.

Kearan didn't dare look round – he just ran back
down to the other pirates
to tell them what had happened.

Meanwhile, the 'ghost' giggled to herself. This was fun!

"**She's here,**" spluttered Kearan.
"**Who's** here?" said Captain Codeye.
"Th-th-the ghost of Pinkbeard!"
"Don't be silly Kearan, you know there are no
such things as ghosts," scoffed Captain Codeye.
"But Daisy saw her too," said Kearan.

"Hmmm,"
thought Captain Codeye.
He took his torch
and went to investigate.

Captain Codeye went to the bow of the ship. Suddenly a ghostly figure appeared right in front of him.

"Ahhh!"

he screamed, and ran as fast as he could back to the pirates. "I-I-I think the ghost of Pinkbeard is real after all," he chattered.

"What's all the shouting about?"
asked Maisey.

"Sh-sh-she's here," they gabbled. "We've all seen
the ghost of Pinkbeard here on our ship."

Maisey looked thoughtful.
Then she spotted
something familiar lying on the deck.
"That's Milly's headscarf,"
she said.

"I think I know what's going on here,"
she whispered. "Look, there she is!"

The pirates crept up to where Milly was hiding.

"BOO!" they shouted, all together.
Poor Milly nearly jumped out of her skin.

"Ohhhh, please don't be angry with me,
ghost pirates," she squeaked.
"I won't steal your ghost treasure, I promise.

I'm just a tiny little pirate!"

All the pirates burst out laughing.

"That was NOT funny," said Milly, when she realised
they were not the ghost pirates after all.
After all their adventures, the pirates decided
it was time to go home.

"But wait – look!" said Milly, pointing out to sea.
"It's true, there really is a ghost ship."
"Milly," groaned the pirates, "Don't be silly,
we're not falling for that one again."

So, they all sailed home to bed,
ready for another big adventure on the seven seas.